KNOCK KNOCK
MY DAD'S DREAM FOR ME

BY DANIEL BEATY • ILLUSTRATED BY BRYAN COLLIER

Little, Brown and Company
New York • Boston

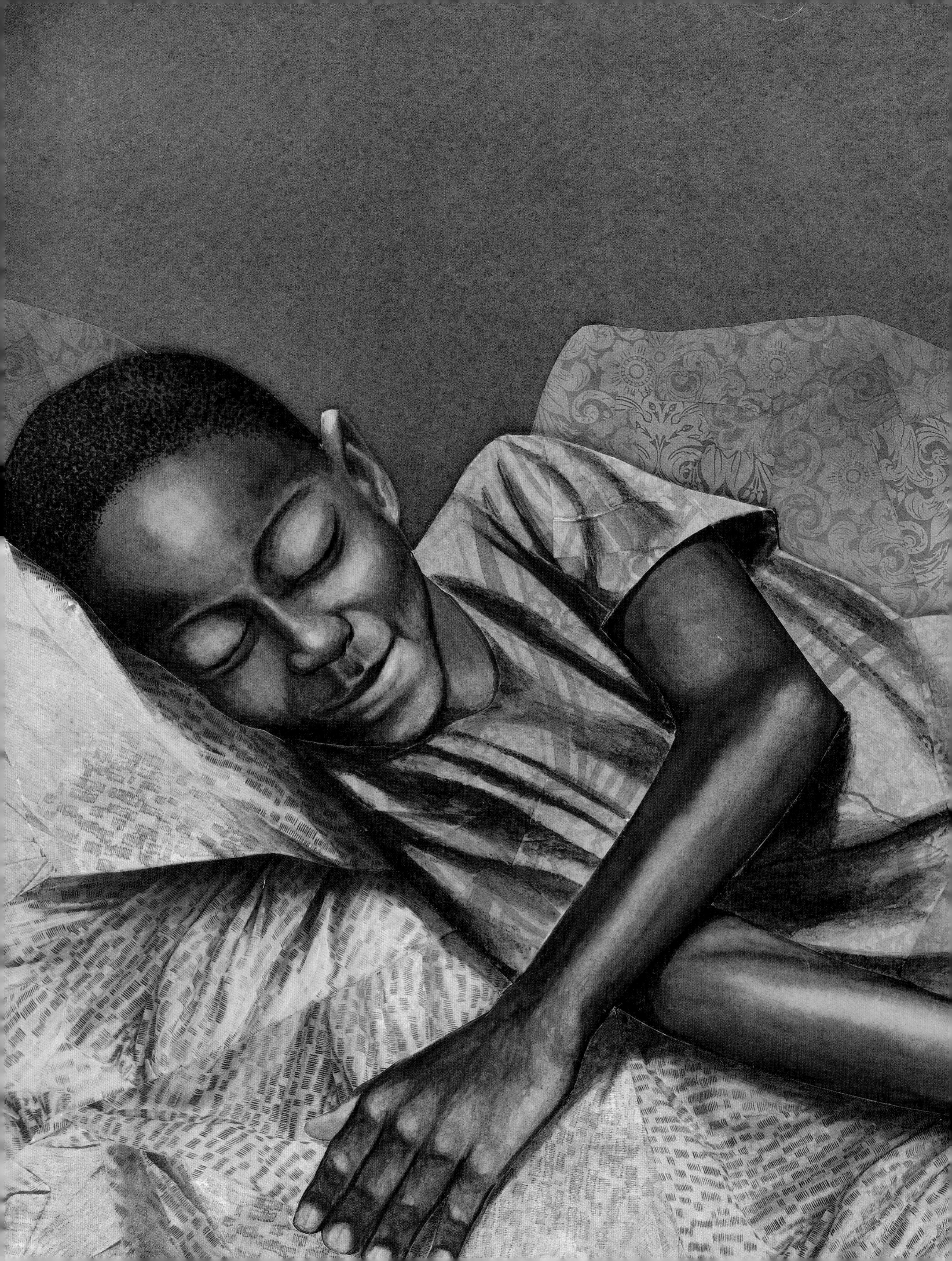

Every morning, I play a game with my father.
He goes KNOCK KNOCK on my door,
and I pretend to be asleep
till he gets right next to the bed.
Then I get up and jump into his arms.
"Good morning, Papa!"

And my papa, he tells me, "I love you."
We share a game...KNOCK KNOCK.

And then one day the knock never comes.
I wait, but Papa's not there to play our game.

And morning after morning he never comes.

He never comes to help me get ready for school.

He never comes to cook my favorite scrambled eggs.
He never comes to help me with my homework after school.

I listen at the door, but I never hear his knock....
And then I think, *Maybe he comes when I'm not home.*
So I decide to write him a letter and leave it on my desk:
"Papa, come home, 'cause I miss you,
miss you waking me in the mornings and telling me you love me.

"Papa, come home, 'cause there are things I don't know,
and when I get older I thought you could teach me
how to dribble a ball, how to shave...

"...how to drive, how to fix the car.

"Papa, come home, 'cause I want to be just like you,
but I'm forgetting who you are."

Two whole months pass,
and my letter to my papa still sits on my desk,
but I leave it and wait for my papa's knock.

And then one day I come home from school,
and on my desk, I find a letter from my father:

TO MY Dear Son

"Dear Son,
Ask your mama to help you make
those scrambled eggs we love.
Remember to do your homework
before you watch TV.

"I am sorry I will not be coming home.

"For every lesson I will not be there to teach you, hear these words:

"As you grow older, shave in one direction with strong, deliberate strokes to avoid irritation.

"No longer will I be there to knock on your door,
so you must learn to knock for yourself.

"KNOCK KNOCK down the doors that I could not.

"KNOCK KNOCK
to open new doors to your dreams.

"KNOCK KNOCK for me,
for as long as you become your best,
the best of me still lives in you.

"KNOCK KNOCK with the knowledge that you are my son and you have a bright, beautiful future.

"For despite my absence you are still here.

"KNOCK KNOCK.

Who's there?

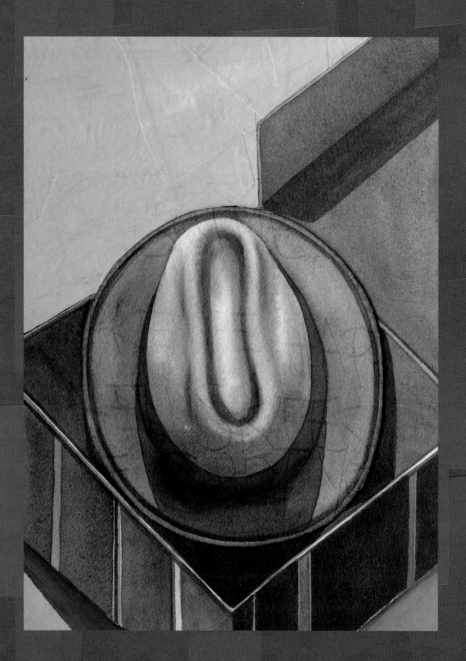

"You are."

AUTHOR'S NOTE

When I was a small child, my father was my principal caregiver. While my mother was at the office working, my father would change my diapers, feed me, and let me ride on his shoulders to the grocery store. He also woke me up each morning with our private Knock Knock game. When I was three, he was incarcerated. My mother took me to visit him in prison, and he was behind glass. This experience was traumatic for me, and I was not allowed to visit my father again in prison for many years. As I grew older, I became aware of the tremendous void created by my father's absence. On my journey to adulthood, I realized how important it was for me to address the pain created by this separation. Later, as an educator of small children, I discovered how many of my students were also dealing with the loss of a father from incarceration, divorce, or sometimes even death. This experience prompted me to tell the story of this loss from a child's perspective and also to offer hope that every fatherless child can still create the most beautiful life possible.

—Daniel Beaty

ILLUSTRATOR'S NOTE

I was inspired by the incredible monologue "Knock Knock" by Daniel Beaty when I saw it performed. His emotional delivery and the moving text of a boy's struggles to navigate his way toward manhood—not completely alone but without the presence of his father—help set an emotional tone for the journey.

The art is created in watercolor and collage, and starts with the boy full of joy and light as he plays the Knock Knock game with his father. When his father is no longer there, the boy's rainbow falls, and his world crumbles beneath his feet. The sky in the art is not so blue, which symbolizes the boy's loss. But as we fast-forward well into his manhood, the boy's days get better. However, he still longs for his father's presence.

I connect with this story because it speaks to me as a son and a father, and I'm moved by the loss this child experiences without his father present to help answer life's questions about how to trust and love and become whole. These are universal themes that are not bound by race, socioeconomic status, or gender. This book is not just about loss, but also about hope, making healthy choices, and not letting our past define our future.

—Bryan Collier

To my mother, Shirley Magee. Thank you for being
both mother and father.
—D.B.

To all parents, guardians, and extended family
who continue to love and lead our little ones.
—B.C.

About This Book

This book was edited by Alvina Ling and designed by
Stephanie Bart-Horvath under the art direction of Patti Ann Harris.
The production was supervised by Jonathan Lopes, and the
production editor was Christine Ma.

The illustrations for this book were done in watercolor and
collage on 400-pound Arches watercolor paper. The book was
printed on 128-gsm Gold Sun matte paper. The text was set in
Gotham, and the display type is Hatmaker.

Text copyright © 2013 by Daniel Beaty • Illustrations copyright © 2013 by Bryan Collier
All rights reserved. In accordance with the U.S. Copyright Act of 1976, the scanning, uploading, and electronic
sharing of any part of this book without the permission of the publisher is unlawful piracy and theft of the author's
intellectual property. If you would like to use material from the book (other than for review purposes), prior written
permission must be obtained by contacting the publisher at permissions@hbgusa.com. Thank you for your support
of the author's rights. • Little, Brown and Company • Hachette Book Group • 237 Park Avenue, New York, NY
10017 • Visit our website at www.lb-kids.com • Little, Brown and Company is a division of Hachette Book Group,
Inc. • The Little, Brown name and logo are trademarks of Hachette Book Group, Inc. • The publisher is not
responsible for websites (or their content) that are not owned by the publisher. • First Edition: December 2013 •
Library of Congress Cataloging-in-Publication Data • Beaty, Daniel. • Knock knock: my dad's dream for me / by
Daniel Beaty ; illustrated by Bryan Collier.—First edition. • pages cm. • Summary: "A boy wakes up one morning to
find his father gone. At first, he feels lost. But his father has left him a letter filled with advice to guide him through
the times he cannot be there"—Provided by publisher. • ISBN 978-0-316-20917-5 • [1. Fathers and sons—Fiction.
2. Separation (Psychology)—Fiction. 3. African Americans—Fiction.] I. Collier, Bryan, illustrator. II. Title. •
PZ7.B3805475Kn 2014 • [E]—dc23 • 2012043088 • 10 9 8 7 6 5 4 3 2 1 • SC • Printed in China